Stranger Than Fiction

WILD ENGINEERING

By Virginia Loh-Hagan

Disclaimer: This series focuses on the strangest of the strange. Have fun reading about strange people and things! But please do not try any of the antics in this book. Be safe and smart!

45th Parallel Press

Published in the United States of America by Cherry Lake Publishing
Ann Arbor, Michigan
www.cherrylakepublishing.com

Reading Adviser: Marla Conn MS, Ed., Literacy specialist, Read-Ability, Inc.

Photo Credits: © E_Sh/Shutterstock.com, cover: © NASA, 1, 5, 28, 29, 30; © David Straub/Shutterstock.com, 6; ©Mike Householder/ASSOCIATED PRESS, 7; ©Willyam Bradberry/Shutterstock.com, 8; ©Charles Krupa/ASSOCIATED PRESS, 9; © SolStock/iStock.com, 10; © Dabarti CGI/Shutterstock.com, 12; © science photo/Shutterstock.com, 13; © wong yu liang/Shutterstock.com, 14; © Nejron Photo/Shutterstock.com, 15; © Greatandaman/dreamstime.com, 16; © OLOS / Shutterstock.com, 17; © andriano_cz/iStock.com, 18; © Geasuha/Shutterstock.com, 20; © Tempura/iStock.com, 21; © Josemaria Toscano/Shutterstock.com, 22; © nickehallgren/iStock.com, 23; © Guido Akster/Shutterstock.com, 24; © E_Sh/Shutterstock.com, 25; © alxcrs/Shutterstock.com, 26; © Alexey_Arz/Shutterstock.com, 27

Graphic Element Credits: ©saki80/Shutterstock.com, back cover, front cover, multiple interior pages; ©queezz/Shutterstock.com, back cover, front cover, multiple interior pages; ©Ursa Major/Shutterstock.com, front cover, multiple interior pages; ©Zilu8/Shutterstock.com, multiple interior pages

45th Parallel Press is an imprint of Cherry Lake Publishing.

Library of Congress Cataloging-in-Publication Data has been filed and is available at catalog.loc.gov

Printed in the United States of America
Corporate Graphics

About the Author

Dr. Virginia Loh-Hagan is an author, university professor, former classroom teacher, and curriculum designer. She wrote books about engineering feats for Cherry Lake Publishing. She lives in San Diego with her very tall husband and very naughty dogs.

Table of Contents

Introduction

Engineers design. They build. They fix. They create. They work on buildings. They work on machines. They work on engines. They think about math. They think about science. They think about art.

They do amazing **feats**. They build great **marvels**! Feats and marvels are skillful or daring accomplishments. Engineers make things happen. They solve problems. They think outside the box. They make the impossible possible.

There's strange engineering. And then, there's really strange engineering. Some engineering feats are super strange. They're so strange that they're hard to believe. They sound like fiction. But these stories are all true!

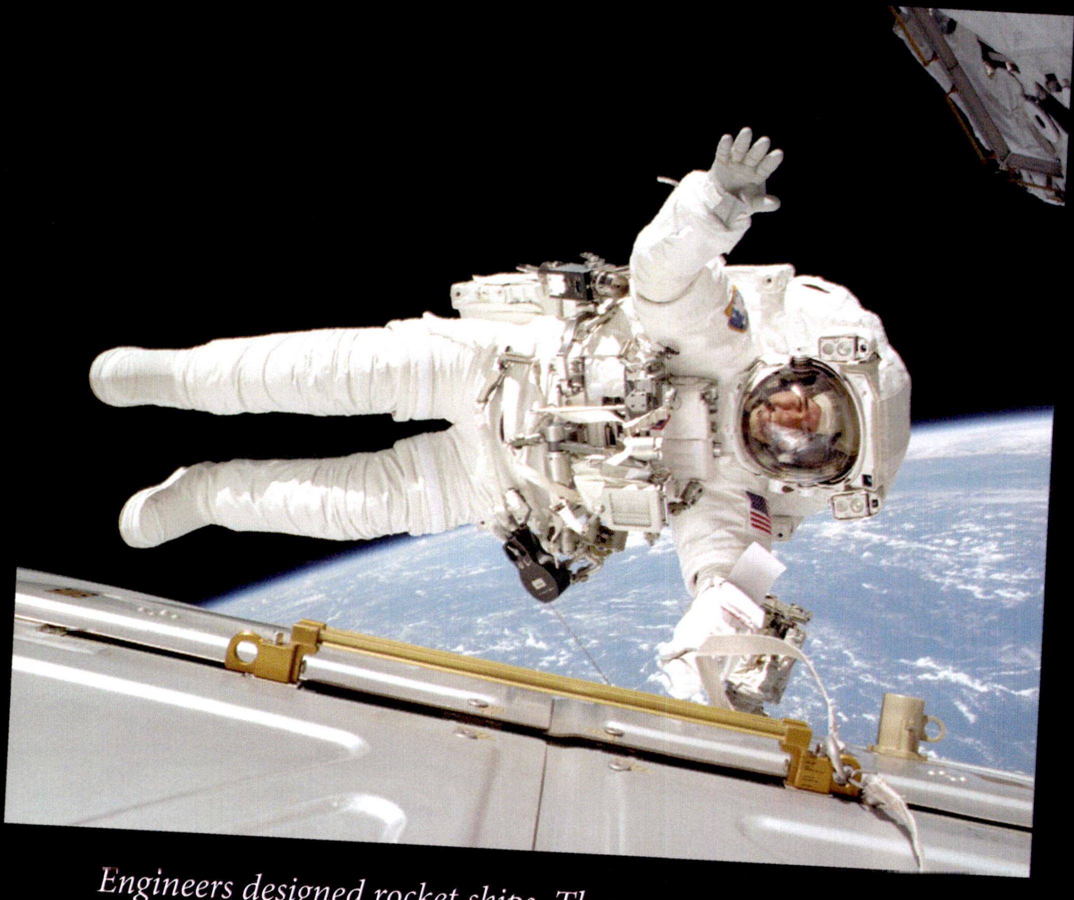

Engineers designed rocket ships. They sent man to the moon.

chapter one

Moving Nature

Engineers moved a big oak tree. The tree is 65 feet (20 meters) tall. It weighs 700,000 pounds (317,515 kilograms). It's 250 years old. It was in front of the University of Michigan's School of Business. The school building was being **expanded**. Expand means to make bigger.

The tree needed to be moved or cut down. Students fought for the tree. People gave money to help. They paid $400,000 to move the tree.

Metal pipes were placed underneath it. Big air bags were put under the tree. The tree was lifted from the ground.

Engineers use simple machines and tools.

Trailers were placed under it. The tree was rolled. An air bag busted. But it was fixed. The tree was moved 300 feet (91 m). It's doing well. It grew new roots. It grew new leaves.

chapter two

Animal Robots

German engineers made a "**bionic** kangaroo." Bionic means having both living and machine parts. This robot moves like a kangaroo. It saves energy from each jump. It uses the energy for the next jump. It can keep jumping. It doesn't get tired. It jumps almost 3 feet (1 m) high. Real kangaroos save and reuse energy. They use their leg muscles. Their legs are like springs.

U.S. engineers made a robot cheetah. Most robots are slow. They're heavy. The robot cheetah runs as fast as humans. It can

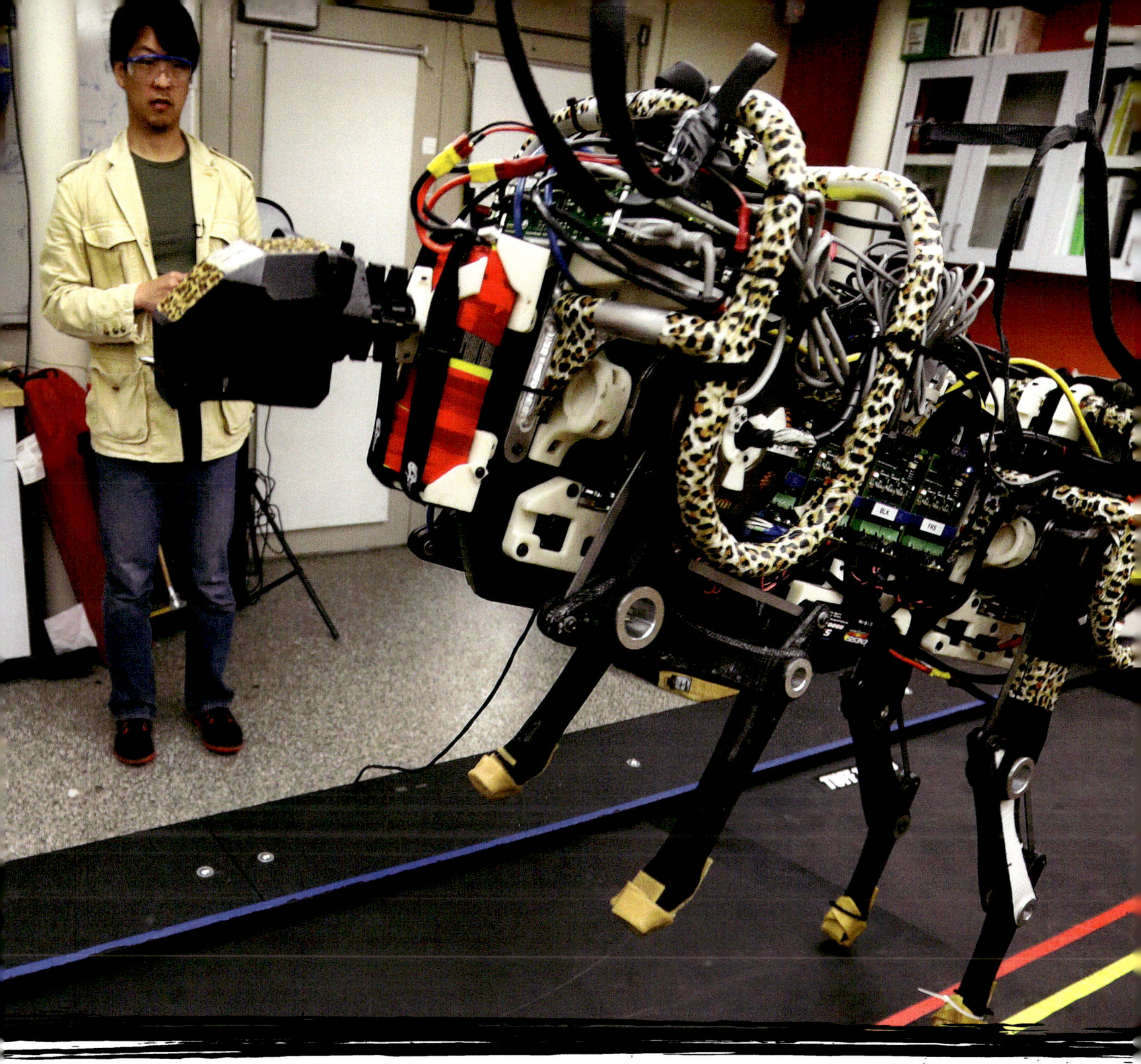

Robots can do things humans can't.

see things. It can walk around things. It can jump over things. It can go upstairs. It can balance on three legs.

Harvard is a top university. It's in Massachusetts. Harvard engineers built the first **hybrid** robot animal. Hybrid is a thing made by combining two elements.

Harvard engineers made a stingray. The stingray is small. It's the size of a coin. It has a gold skeleton. Its skin is made of rat heart cells. It can move. Engineers use light to control it. They flash lights. More flashing makes the robot move faster. Shining lights make it turn on one side.

Stingrays move like beating hearts. Engineers want to make bionic hearts. An engineer said, "One day we can use this technology to rebuild parts of the human body."

Engineers and scientists work together to solve problems.

Explained by Science

Engineering marvels rely on science. Conservation of energy is a science rule. Conservation means to save. Things move around over time. They have energy. Energy may change forms. But it's conserved. It's saved. The total amount of energy is the same. In other words, energy can't be created or destroyed. It can be transformed from one form to another. Transform means to change. Or energy can be transferred from one thing to another. Transfer means to move. Bowling is an example. A bowling ball knocks over pins. The pins were standing still. They get hit. They fall. Energy is transferred from the ball to the pins. No energy is lost.

chapter three

3D Printing

Printers print more than paper. They print things in **3D**. 3D means three-dimensional. This means they're in real-life form. They're solid. 3D printers make amazing things. They make musical instruments. They make shoes. They make tools. They make fake arms and hands.

Engineers even make cars with 3D printers. They've also made motorcycles. Blade is the name of the car. Dagger is the name of the motorcycle. 3D printers make parts. The parts snap together. They're like linking blocks. This process is **green**. Green means good for the environment. 3D printing makes less trash. It doesn't make bad gases.

3D printing started in the 1980s.

chapter four

Indoor Farm

There was a bad storm in Japan. People went hungry. There was no food. Shigeharu Shimamura is a plant scientist. He wanted to help. He built the world's largest indoor farm. It's 25,000 square feet (2,323 sq m). It has 17,500 special lights. Shimamura controls the temperature. He controls the lights. He makes days and nights shorter. This means food grows more. Food grows faster. The indoor farm grows 10,000 heads of lettuce each day. This is 100 times more than a regular farm.

The indoor farm was built in an old factory.

It's green. It's free of germs. It's free of chemicals. It makes less waste. It uses less water. It uses less power. In the future, robots will do all the farmwork.

chapter five

Elevators

The Bailong Elevator is in China. It's also called the Hundred Dragons Elevator. It's an outdoor elevator. It's the highest. It's over 1,000 feet (305 m) high. It's the heaviest. It's built off the side of a big cliff. It's in a national forest park.

It's made of thick glass. People can see sights as they ride up and down. It takes 2 minutes to ride from bottom to top. It carries 50 people at a time. It carries 4,000 people per hour. It carries 18,000 people a day. It goes over 16 feet (5 m) per second.

It would take close to 3 hours to walk up to the top if you skipped taking the elevator.

Elevators take up a lot of room. They're carried by ropes. The ropes bring them up and down. This limits how high they can go. This means people can't build as tall as they'd like. It means they can't build as wide as they'd like.

German engineers are working on this. They're building special elevators. The elevators are called MULTI. This means many. These elevators go up and down. They also go left to right. And they go diagonally. They move on tracks with magnets. They go over 1,000 feet (305 m) per minute. They were tested in Germany. They were tested in a tower.

Speeds over 2,000 feet (610 m) per minute cause ear problems and sickness.

Spotlight Biography

Kim Ung-yong was born in 1962. He's South Korean. He's an engineer. He has a world record. He has the highest IQ. IQ measures how smart someone is. Kim's score was 210. A normal score is around 100. Kim started speaking at 6 months. He could read several languages by age 2. He wrote books and poems by age 4. He solved hard math problems by age 5. He started college at age 3. He studied engineering. He got his doctorate. He worked at NASA at age 8. He worked there for 10 years. He said, "I led my life like a machine." He was lonely. He missed his mother. He went back to South Korea. He wanted to be a regular person. He's now very happy.

chapter six

Millau Viaduct

Viaducts are bridges. They span over land. The Millau Viaduct is in France. It's the highest bridge in Europe. Its deck is over 900 feet (274 m) from the ground. It's the tallest bridge in the world. It's 1,125 feet (343 m) tall. It glides above the clouds. It's over 8,000 feet (2,438 m) wide.

The Millau Viaduct is the longest **cable** bridge. Cables are thick, strong ropes. They hang from the towers. They support the bridge deck.

The bridge has seven tall towers. Each tower weighs 700 tons. The bridge has

The Millau Viaduct took 3 years to build.

seven sails. The sails look like they're floating across the valley. It's a beautiful bridge. It's also a helpful bridge. It eases traffic.

Chapter Seven

Skywalk

People go to Skywalk. They feel like they're walking on clouds. Skywalk is in Arizona. It's in the Grand Canyon. It's a special walkway. It's over 4,000 feet (1,219 m) high. It's 65 feet (20 m) wide. It extends about 70 feet (21 m) from the cliff's edge. It extends out from the side of a canyon. It's U-shaped. It's made of 1 million pounds (453,592 kg) of steel. It's made of 83,000 pounds (37,648 kg) of glass. Its floor is made of glass. The floor weighs over 80,000 pounds (36,287 kg).

Skywalk is strong. It can hold a lot of people. It's built to handle tough winds. It's built to handle earthquakes.

Skywalk is owned by the Hualapai Indian tribe.

chapter eight

Palm Islands

The Palm Islands are **man-made**. Nature didn't make them. Engineers did. The Palm Islands are the world's largest fake islands. They're in Dubai. They're in the Persian Gulf.

Ships **dredged** up sand. Dredge means to scoop up. Builders filled the seabed with sand. They sprayed sand on top. They made a rising surface. They shaped the islands into a palm tree. They piled mountain rock around the islands. The rocks formed a crescent shape. They protected the islands from waves and storms.

The Palm Islands added 320 miles (515 km) of beach.

Builders tried to help sea life. They dropped two jets on the seafloor. The jets became reefs.

chapter nine

Aerial Adventure Park

Adventure parks take up a lot of land. So, engineers built up. They created an **aerial** adventure park. Aerial means in the air. The first park is in Australia. The park is 85 feet (26 m) tall. It's 131 feet (40 m) wide. It has 120 challenges. It has rope bridges. It has swings. It has zip lines. It has free falls. It has beams. It has bouncing pads.

It's safe to move around. It has a walkway. It has stairs. It has a view from the top. There are no nets. People wear straps. They hang from ropes. They float in the air. They feel free. If they fall, they just climb back up.

The aerial park in Australia is a four-level climbing adventure.

chapter ten

International Space Station

The International Space Station (ISS) is a large **spacecraft**. Spacecraft is a machine that travels through space. The ISS **orbits** Earth. Orbit means to circle. The ISS's path is 220 miles (354 km) above Earth. The ISS orbits Earth every 90 minutes. It travels over 17,000 miles (27,359 km) per hour.

Many countries worked together to build it. The ISS is made of many pieces. It was built in space. It was built while moving. Each piece was taken to space. Russia made the first piece. They launched it in 1998. More pieces were added. This happened over many years. The ISS was finished in 2011.

The ISS has science labs from the United States, Russia, Japan, and Europe.

It's a science lab. **NASA** uses it to learn about space. NASA manages the United States' space programs. Six **astronauts** can live in the ISS. Astronauts are space scientists. They travel to space. They use a Russian shuttle to get there. The ISS is big. It's like a house. It has five bedrooms. It has two bathrooms. It has a gym. It has a big window. It has working spaces. It has labs.

It has **solar** panels. Solar means sun. These panels collect sun energy. Sunlight is turned into electricity. Robot arms are attached outside. These arms helped build the ISS. They move astronauts around outside. They help with science tests. Engineers designed the ISS to be very useful.

The ISS is the size of a football field.

Try This!

- Talk to engineers. Ask them what they do. Ask them how they come up with ideas.
- Take a walk. Make a list of engineering feats. Examples are bridges and stadiums.
- Build something. Make a plan. Get the materials. Create a plan of action.
- Learn more about a famous engineer. Make a timeline of the person's life. Include important engineering feats.
- Take a STEM class. STEM stands for Science, Technology, Engineering, and Math.
- Make a simple machine. Examples are catapults or pulleys.
- Make a robot. Enter a robotics contest.
- Do an online search. Look for engineering challenges. Do one of them. Work with your friends.

Consider This!

Take a Position! People who work on computers are called engineers. Some people don't think they're "real" engineers. Do you think they're engineers? Argue your point with reasons and evidence.

Say What? There are different types of engineers. Learn more about them. Compare two types. Explain how they're the same. Explain how they're different.

Think About It! Engineers try to make life better. They try to make it easier. Think of an engineering feat. Learn more about it. Think about how it works.

Learn More!

- Hunt, Shannon, and James Gulliver Hancock. *Engineered! Engineering Design at Work*. Toronto: Kids Can Press, 2017.
- Macaulay, David, and Neil Ardley. *The Way Things Work Now: From Levers to Lasers, Windmills to Wi-Fi, a Visual Guide to the World of Machines*. Boston: Houghton Mifflin Harcourt, 2016.
- Martin, Steve, and Nastia Sleptsova. *Engineer Academy: Are You Ready for the Challenge?* Brighton, UK: Ivy Kids, 2017.

Glossary

aerial (AIR-ee-uhl) in the air

astronauts (AS-truh-nawts) scientists who travel to space

bionic (bye-ON-ik) having both living and machine parts

cable (KAY-buhl) thick, strong rope

dredged (DREJD) scooped up and out

engineers (en-juh-NEERZ) skilled people who design, build, or maintain engines, machines, and buildings

expanded (ik-SPAN-did) extended, added, made bigger

feats (FEETS) daring or skillful accomplishments

green (GREEN) being friendly to the environment

hybrid (HYE-brid) a thing made by combining two elements

man-made (MAN-MAYD) made by man, not by nature

marvels (MAHR-vuhlz) marvelous accomplishments

NASA (NAS-uh) an agency called the National Aeronautics and Space Administration that is in charge of the United States' space program

orbits (OR-bits) circles around

solar (SOH-ler) of the sun

spacecraft (SPAYS-kraft) vehicle that is designed to travel through space

3D (THREE-DEE) three-dimensional, real-life form, solid

viaducts (VYE-uh-duhkts) bridges that span over land

Index